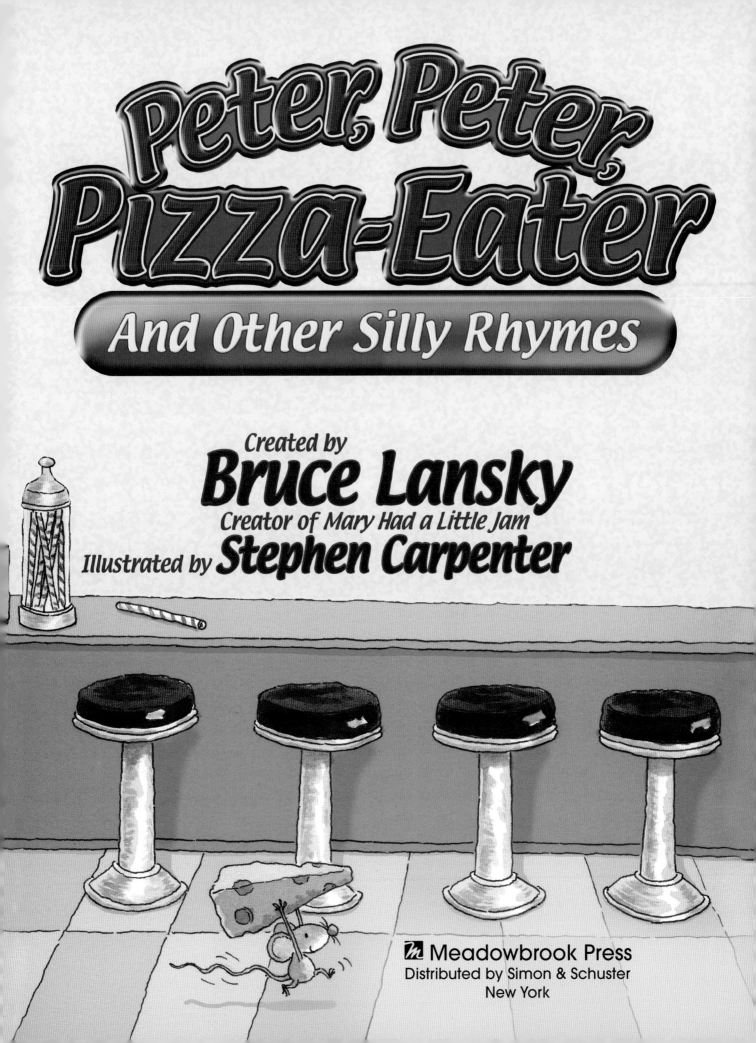

Peter, Peter, Pizza-Eater

And Other Silly Rhymes

Created by
Bruce Lansky
Creator of *Mary Had a Little Jam*

Illustrated by **Stephen Carpenter**

Meadowbrook Press
Distributed by Simon & Schuster
New York

Library of Congress Cataloging-in-Publication Data

Lansky, Bruce.
    Peter, Peter, pizza-eater : and other silly rhymes / created by Bruce Lansky ; illustrated by Stephen Carpenter.
      p. cm.
    Summary: "A collection of silly nursery rhymes that put funny new twists on traditional Mother Goose subjects"—Provided by publisher.
    ISBN 0-88166-490-1 (Meadowbrook Press) ISBN 0-684-03166-3 (Simon & Schuster)
    1. Children's poetry, American. 2. Mother Goose—Adaptations. 3. Nursery rhymes, American. I. Carpenter, Stephen. II. Title.
    PS3562.A564P48 2006
    811'.54—dc22

                    2005007418

Editorial Director: Christine Zuchora-Walske
Coordinating Editor and Copyeditor: Angela Wiechmann
Production Manager: Paul Woods
Graphic Design Manager: Tamara Peterson
Illustrations and Cover Art: Stephen Carpenter

© 2006 by Meadowbrook Creations

Published by Meadowbrook Press, 5451 Smetana Drive, Minnetonka, Minnesota 55343

www.meadowbrookpress.com

BOOK TRADE DISTRIBUTION by Simon and Schuster, a division of Simon and Schuster, Inc., 1230 Avenue of the Americas, New York, New York 10020

10 09 08 07 06   10 9 8 7 6 5 4 3 2 1

Printed in China

Credits

"Blow Your Nose!" (p. 17) copyright © 2000 by Bruce Lansky, first published in *If Pigs Could Fly…and Other Deep Thoughts*; "Diddle Diddle Dumpling" (p. 29) copyright © 2006 by Mark Benthall; "Georgie Porgie, Handsome Guy" (p. 23) copyright © 2006 by Bruce Lansky; "Georgie Porgie, Pudding and Pie" (p. 23) copyright © 2006 by Kenn Nesbitt; "Georgie Porgie—What a Guy!" (p. 23) copyright © 2006 by Robert Scotellaro; "Here Is the Church" (p. 9) copyright © 2006 by Jeff Mondak; "Hey, Diddle, Diddle" (p. 30) copyright © 2006 by Bruce Lansky; "Hickory, Dickory, Dock" (p. 11) copyright © 1994 by Robert Scotellaro, first published in *A Bad Case of the Giggles*; "House Rule" (p. 26) copyright © 2000 by Bruce Lansky, first published in *If Pigs Could Fly…and Other Deep Thoughts*; "Humpty Dumpty" (p. 27) copyright © 2006 by A. Maria Plover; "Humpty Dumpty Sat on the Pot" (p. 26) copyright © 2005 by Linda Knaus, first published in *Tinkle, Tinkle, Little Tot*; "Jack and Jill" (p. 20) copyright © 2006 by Marilyn Helmer; "Jack's Latest Trick" (p. 15) copyright © 2006 by Marilyn Helmer; "Jack Be Nimble" (p. 15) copyright © 2006 by Tim Tocher; "Little Boy Blue" (p. 16) copyright © 2006 by Darren Sardelli; "Little Boy Blue" (p. 10) copyright © 2006 by Graham Denton; "Lyndon's Hair Is Falling Down" (p. 22) copyright © 2006 by Bruce Lansky; "Mary Had a Little Dog" (p. 6) copyright © 2006 by Bruce Lansky; "Mary Had a Little Frog" (p. 31) copyright © 2006 by Bruce Lansky; "Mary Had a Little Ham" (p. 25) copyright © 1994 by Bruce Lansky, first published in *A Bad Case of the Giggles*; "Mary Had a Little Mouse" (p. 25) copyright © 2006 by Bruce Lansky; "Mary Had a Little Mouse" (p. 7) copyright © 2006 by Joyce Armor; "Mary Had a Little Pet" (p. 7) copyright © 2006 by Judith Natelli McLaughlin; "Old Mother Hubbard" (p. 24) copyright © 2006 by Dave Crawley; "Peter Piper Painted Pickles" (p. 22) copyright © 2006 by Bruce Lansky; "Peter, Peter, Pizza-Eater" (p. 5) copyright © 2006 by Bruce Lansky; "Rockin' Diddle, Diddle" (p. 30) copyright © 2006 by Helen Ksypka; "Row, Row, Row Your Boat" (p. 21) copyright © 1994 by Bill Dodds, first published in *A Bad Case of the Giggles*; "Row, Row, Row Your Boat" (p. 20) copyright © 2006 by Bruce Lansky; "Rub-a-Dub-Dub" (p. 28) copyright © 2006 by Linda Knaus; "Sing a Song of Six Cents" (p. 24) copyright © 2006 by Bruce Lansky; "There Was an Odd Lady" (p. 18) copyright © 2006 by Bruce Lansky; "There Was an Old Lady" (p. 12) copyright © 2006 by Bruce Lansky; "There Was an Old Lady" (p. 19) copyright © 2006 by Bruce Lansky; "There Was an Old Woman" (p. 19) copyright © 1994 by Bill Dodds, first published in *A Bad Case of the Giggles*; "Tinkle, Tinkle, Little Bat" (p. 32) copyright © 2004 by Dianne Rowley, first published in *Rolling in the Aisles*; "Yankee Doodle" (p. 14) copyright © 2006 by Linda Knaus; "Yankee Doodle Flew through Space" (p. 14) copyright © 2006 by Bruce Lansky; "Yankee Doodle's Nose Is Running" (p. 14) copyright © 2000 by Bruce Lansky, first published in *If Pigs Could Fly…and Other Deep Thoughts*. All rhymes used by permission of the authors.

Acknowledgments

We'd like to thank the following families and classes for taking time to help us select the rhymes in this collection: Peggy and Tommy Boehm; Cathy and Kayla Chelgren; Linda Cohen and children at Shalom Yeladim Preschool; Linda Coleman, Connie Mikelson, Dawn Sailer, Sheri Simpson, Tracy Thomson, and students at Deephaven Elementary; Michelle, Grant, and Greta Gustafson Delaune; Roxanne, Bjorn, and Trygve Eggen; Julie Anne, Anna, and Tate Engleson; Missy and Katrina Flettre; Deb, Brett, and Samantha Flettre; Darrell, Sheila, and Austin Gaffke; Sue Grande and family; Colleen, Kierney, and Addison Gray; Joe Gredler, Jane Davidson, and Olivia and Isabel Gredler; Carla and Matthew Johnson; Jessica, Aaron, and Emma Klaustermeier; Jennifer and Alexis Kretsch; Kristin Kuehn, Georgia Rasmus, and students at Groveland Elementary; Brenda and Royce Lund; Julie and Katelyn Magnan; Elaine and Walker Matthew; Megan, James, and Julia McGough; Darlene, Alexis, and Cade Mueller; Lesa and Jack Nugent; Valeka and Jeremy Petersen; Tami, Anna, and Emily Peterson; Jamie, Wes, Athena, and Will Pogue; Martin, Sr., Lori, Martin, Jr., and Maguire Radosevic; Lisa and Hayley Robinson; Jill, Zachary, and Gabrielle Rome; Kelly and Nick Schurgl; Nancy and Angus Stoddart; Glenda Streeter and children at Happy Hearts Daycare; Lisa, Jay, and Rachel Tarbell; Amanda Vaith and Logan Adams; Kathy and Evan Vargas; Brenda and Maya Walther; and Lew and Toni Watson and Taylor Pirozzolo. We'd also like to thank Kate Knight with KrazyPets, Inc., for help with testing.

Contents

Peter, Peter, pizza-eater,
How I wish that you were neater.
Half the pizza's on your shirt.
Clean the mess, or no dessert.

Mary had a little dog.
Its fur was black as night.
And everyone that Mary met
The dog was sure to bite.

It followed her to school one day,
Which was against the rule.
The dog bit Mary's teacher's leg.
They threw her out of school.

Mary had some bubble gum.
She chewed it long and slow.
And everywhere that Mary went
Her gum was sure to blow.

She chewed the gum in school one day,
Which was against the rule.
The teacher took her pack away
And chewed it after school.

Mary had a little mouse.
Its fur was white as snow.
And everywhere that Mary went
The mouse was sure to go.

It followed her to school one day,
Which wasn't Mary's plan,
For when the mouse jumped on her desk,
The teacher screamed and ran!

Mary had a little pet.
Its fur was black as night.
It followed her to school one day,
Which gave the kids a fright.

It made the teachers shout and scream.
It gave them such a scare.
For Mary didn't have a lamb—
She had a grizzly bear.

Here is the church and here is the steeple.
Open the doors and see all the people.
Preacher is talking and cell phones are beeping.
None of this noise can keep Daddy from sleeping.

Little Boy Blue, come mow the lawn—
There's no one else to do it.
The sheep's in the meadow, the cow's in the corn,
And both refuse to chew it!

Hickory, dickory, dock!
A goat just ate my sock,
Then took my shirt
For his dessert.
Hickory, dickory, dock!

There was an old lady who lived in a zoo.
She never got bored; she had so much to do.

She climbed with the monkeys. She swam with the eels.
She talked to the parrots and played with the seals.

The old lady's happy; she never gets blue.
And that's why she'll never move back to a shoe.

Yankee Doodle flew through space,
Riding on a rocket.
He landed on the moon and brought
Green cheese back in his pocket.

Yankee Doodle went to town
To buy some macaroni.
He had to ride a poodle 'cuz
He couldn't find a pony.

Yankee Doodle went to town
With his baby blankie.
Every time he blew his nose
He used it for a hankie.

Jack showed off
His latest trick:
He jumped over
A candlestick.
But Jack must learn
To jump much higher
So his pants
Won't catch on fire!

Jack be nimble, Jack be quick.
Your friend's about to play a trick.
Jack was sluggish, Jack was slow.
A squirt gun soaked him head to toe.

Little Boy Blue,
Please cover your nose.
You sneezed on Miss Muffet
And ruined her clothes.
You sprayed Mother Hubbard,
And now she is sick.
You put out the fire
On Jack's candlestick.
Your sneeze is the reason
Why Humpty fell down.
You drenched Yankee Doodle
When he came to town.
The blind mice are angry!
The sheep are upset!
From now on use tissues
So no one gets wet!

Little Boy Blue,
Please blow your nose.
It drips like a faucet
And sprays like a hose.
Your brother and sister
Are getting upset,
So please blow your nose—
'Cause you're getting them wet!

There was an odd lady
Who lived in a shoe,
Which, I think you'll agree,
Is an odd thing to do.
Her kids and her dogs
And her cats ran away.
The shoe was so small;
There was no room to play.

There was an old lady who lived in a tree.
She changed in the bushes so no one could see.
And while she was sleeping, the branches would shake.
Her snoring was keeping the birdies awake.

There was an old woman
Who lived in a shoe;
With so many children,
What else could she do?

Their home had no windows,
No doors, and no locks—
The kids were all happy
But smelled like old socks.

Jack and Jill
Went up the hill
Riding on a pony.
They had a picnic
At the top
With cheese and macaroni.

Row, row, row your boat
Gently up the creek.
You might get your bottom wet
If you spring a leak.

Row, row, row your boat
Gently down the stream,
Until you hit the waterfall—
Then you'll start to scream.

Lyndon's hair is falling down,
Falling down, falling down.
Lyndon's buzzcut makes him frown.
He's unhappy.

Lyndon's hair is on the floor,
On the floor, on the floor.
He is walking out the door
With a hat on.

Peter Piper painted pickles
    Purple, red, and pink.
He discovered painting pickles
    Made his paintbrush stink.

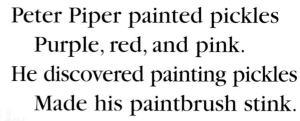

Georgie Porgie—what a guy!—
Kissed the girls and made them cry.
Though his kisses were quite sweet,
He was standing on their feet!

Georgie Porgie, pudding and pie,
Kissed the girls and made them sigh.
He's so cute, they stand in lines
Just to give him valentines.

Georgie Porgie, handsome guy,
Won't kiss the girls, and so they cry.
It breaks their hearts—he loves another.
He's only five; he loves his mother.

Old Mother Hubbard
Went to the cupboard;
She asked her poor dog to wait.
But when she returned,
The old lady learned
That Fido had cleaned off her plate.

Sing a song of six cents,
I wish that I could buy
A candy bar, some bubble gum,
A slice of apple pie.
I'd like a can of cola.
I'd like an ice-cream cone.
There's six cents in my piggy bank—
I'll have to get a loan.

Mary had a little mouse.
Its fur was white as snow.
And everywhere that Mary went
The mouse was sure to go.
It went to Mary's birthday bash,
Which was a big mistake.
While everyone was singing,
The mouse ate Mary's cake.

Mary had a little ham
With scrambled eggs and toast with jam.
Then she had a little cake,
And then she had a bellyache.

Humpty Dumpty sat on the pot.
Humpty Dumpty tinkled a lot.
Now all the king's horses
And all the king's men
Will never dress Humpty in diapers again.

Roses are red,
Violets are blue,
Please flush the toilet
After you're through.

Humpty Dumpty laid by the pool.
Humpty Dumpty thought he was cool.
He wouldn't wear sunscreen.
He thought it was dumb.
Now he's served at McDonalds
With ham on a bun.

Rub-a-dub-dub,
Get back in that tub,
And scrub all your fingers and toes.
You're dirty and smelly.
You're smeared with grape jelly.
And this time, please take off your clothes!

Diddle diddle dumpling, my son John
Went to bed with his blue jeans on.
The poor little guy is out of luck.
He's still in his pants 'cause his
    zipper got stuck!

Hey, diddle, diddle,
The cat played the fiddle.
The cow jumped over the moon.

The cow jumped so high,
He thought he could fly,
But came down at the end
of the tune.

Hey, diddle, diddle,
The cat plays the fiddle.
The cow keeps the beat with a spoon.
On trumpet, there's monkey.
They're hip and they're funky
Whenever they're playin' a tune.

Mary had a little frog.
The frog croaked every day.
And Mary always wondered
What the frog was trying to say.

To freshen up the critter's breath,
She fed the frog some mints.
And when she gave the frog a kiss,
It turned into a prince.

Mary and the prince were wed,
And on that happy day,
Mary asked the prince just what
The frog had tried to say.

"Mary," said the handsome prince,
"I'm going to tell you true:
When the frog croaked it was saying,
'I love you.'"

Tinkle, tinkle, little bat.
Wonder where the potty's at?

Straight ahead or to the right?
Caves are very dark at night.

Little bat, why do you frown?
Did you tinkle upside down?